The Starry Night

Neil Waldman

The Starry Night

Boyds Mills Press

Find out more about *The Starry Night* and how it was created at
www.thestarrynight.com

Text and illustrations copyright © 1999 by Neil Waldman
All rights reserved

Published by Caroline House
Boyds Mills Press, Inc.
A Highlights Company
815 Church Street
Honesdale, Pennsylvania 18431
Printed in China

Publisher Cataloging-in-Publication Data

Waldman, Neil.
The starry night / written and illustrated by Neil Waldman.—1st
ed.
[32]p. : col. ill. ; cm.
Summary: Vincent Van Gogh befriends a young boy in New York City in this
picture book fantasy about art and creativity.
ISBN 1-56397-736-2
1. Van Gogh, Vincent, 1853-1890—Fiction—Juvenile literature.
2. Fantasy—Juvenile literature. 3. New York(N.Y.)—Fiction—Juvenile
literature. [1. Van Gogh, Vincent , 1853-1890—Fiction. 2. Fantasy
—Fiction.
3. New York(N.Y.)—Fiction] I. Title.
[E]—dc21 1999 AC CIP
Library of Congress Catalog Card Number 98-88217

First edition, 1999
The text of this book is set in 18-point Usherwood Book.
Illustrations are done in oil on canvas, acrylic on canvas, and pen and ink on paper.

10 9 8 7 6 5 4

Visit our website: www.boydsmillspress.com

To the good men and women of the Children's Aid Society,
whose steadfast efforts have enriched the lives of countless
young people in New York.

As a small boy, I stumbled upon the paintings of the Dutch artist Vincent Van Gogh (1853-1890), and they drew me into them like a powerful magnet. I could feel their rich vibrating colors resonating within me as I was swept up in the torrent of Vincent's slashing brushstrokes. I inhaled the wild spectrum of emotion that throbbed within these bold canvases, feeling their pain, sadness, excitement, and rapture, but mostly their abundant joy.

When I grew a bit older, I began reading biographies of the painter I had come to love. I cried when I read about the degradation and loneliness that Vincent suffered throughout most of his life. But as I read book after book, it seemed clear to me that something was missing. For although these recountings went on at length about Vincent's fabled suffering, they rarely spoke of the joy I knew he must have felt while painting.

I imagined bringing Vincent to New York and taking him touring through the city of my birth. Although I couldn't have known it at the time, the seeds for this story had been sown.

When I illustrated the book, I decided to use a child's interpretation of "The Starry Night" on the last page of the story. And so I turned to the children of an art class that I teach with the Southern Westchester Board of Cooperative Educational Services. Their drawings may be found on the endpapers, as well as on the final page. The children are Brighid Catherine Moore, Keiji Ishiguri, Barron Bass, Feras Khalbuss, Michelle Princi, Ashley Chin, Nina Quirk-Goldblatt, Juan Carlos Cadavid, Brandon Leonardo, Callan Rogers, and Dean Ferrara. These students come from the following school districts: Eastchester, Elmsford, Greenburgh, Rye Neck, and the Tarrytowns, in Westchester County, New York.

I'd also like to thank my neighbor, Westerfield Tolbert, who posed for me as I sketched the character of Bernard.

Final thanks goes to the wonderful team at Boyds Mills Press, whose dedication and creative vision are reflected in the pages of this volume: Kent Brown (publisher), Larry Rosler (editor), and Tim Gillner (art director).

Across the shaded hills
    and winding pathways of Central Park,
    daffodil stars exploded
    in yellow splendor.

A group of boys
    raced alongside the still reflecting pool,
      where children played with sailboats
        under the watchful eyes of their mothers.

The boys darted around a sharp curve
and ran past a frail-looking man,
who stood before an old wooden easel.

The last of the boys came to a stop
as the others charged off onto a grassy field.
"C'mon, Bernard!" one of them called back,
but Bernard didn't move.

He just stood there staring
at the brightly colored canvas.
The man glanced at Bernard
and returned to his painting.

Bernard sat down in the grass.
After a while, the man turned and nodded.
"It's finished," he said in funny-sounding English.
"The Big Apple never looked better!" Bernard beamed.

The man began packing up his paints and easel.
    "Where are you going?" Bernard asked.
      "To find another place that asks to be painted."
      "What's your name?"

"Vincent."
    The man smiled.
      "Do you paint all the time?"
        "Yes," said Vincent. "That's why I am here."

"Where do you come from?" Bernard asked.
    "Far away. I just arrived today."
      "Well, I've lived here all my life," Bernard said.
      "I could show you some amazing places."
        "I'd like that very much," said Vincent.

Bernard took Vincent north to Harlem,
south to the Statue of Liberty,
and east to the Brooklyn Bridge.

They spent their days in Greenwich Village,

in Chinatown,

in Times Square,
and on Fifth Avenue.

Wherever they went,
Bernard watched
as Vincent painted New York
in bright and beautiful colors.

Then one day Vincent said,
"It's time for me to go.
But before I leave,
there is one place
I want to show you."

Vincent took Bernard to a big building
on Fifty-Third Street.

Inside, the walls were covered with beautiful paintings.
They went up an escalator to the second floor.
Vincent led Bernard to a blue and yellow painting
of a country village at night.

Bernard stood silently for a long time.
He could hardly breathe.
Then he felt a shiver pass through him.

"Vincent, it looks exactly like one of yours!
You painted this picture, didn't you?"
But there was no answer.

"Vincent?"
Bernard spun around,
but Vincent wasn't there.
"Vincent!" he called. "Where are you?"

Bernard raced through every room of the museum,
but his friend was nowhere to be found.
He walked sadly back
to the blue and yellow painting.

Bernard looked at the swirling stars,
    the orange moon,
        and the sleeping village.
He thought about the many days
    when he had watched in wonder
        as Vincent painted the streets of Harlem,
            Midtown,
                the Village,
                    and the great lady with the torch
                        from across the bay in Battery Park.
"The Big Apple never looked so great," Bernard whispered.
    His eyes widened.
        He turned and left the museum.

Bernard came back a few minutes later,
    carrying a brown paper bag.
        He sat down across from Vincent's painting.
Then he opened the bag, took out a sketch pad
    and a box of colored pencils . . .

and Bernard began to draw.

Night